For Dad and Lisa—
storytellers and jungle-lovers
J. H.

For Hal
M. E.

Text copyright © 1994 by Judy Hindley
Illustrations copyright © 1994 by Melanie Epps

First U.S. paperback edition 1996

The Library of Congress has cataloged the hardcover edition as follows:

Hindley, Judy.
Into the jungle / Judy Hindley ; illustrated by Melanie Epps.—1st U.S. ed.
Summary: As they walk softly through the jungle, two children observe
snakes, chimpanzees, a cockatoo, and other animals.
ISBN 1-56402-423-7 (hardcover)
[1. Jungles—Fiction. 2. Jungle animals—Fiction.] I. Epps, Melanie, ill. II. Title.
PZ7.H5696In   1994
[E]—dc20   93-33310
ISBN 0-7636-0021-0 (paperback)

2 4 6 8 10 9 7 5 3 1

Printed in Hong Kong

This book was typeset in Berling.
The pictures were done in oil paint and gesso.

Candlewick Press
2067 Massachusetts Avenue
Cambridge, Massachusetts 02140

INTO the JUNGLE

by
JUDY HINDLEY

illustrated by
MELANIE EPPS

CANDLEWICK PRESS
CAMBRIDGE, MASSACHUSETTS

When you go
into the jungle,
go carefully.

It's a wild place.

In every shadow there could
be a snake curled quietly.
S s s s !

S h h h !
Go carefully.
Walk softly.

Do you hear those
whispery noises up above?

That could be a troop
of chimpanzees.
You'll never see them—
they're too wild and shy.
Wild things never
look you in the eye.

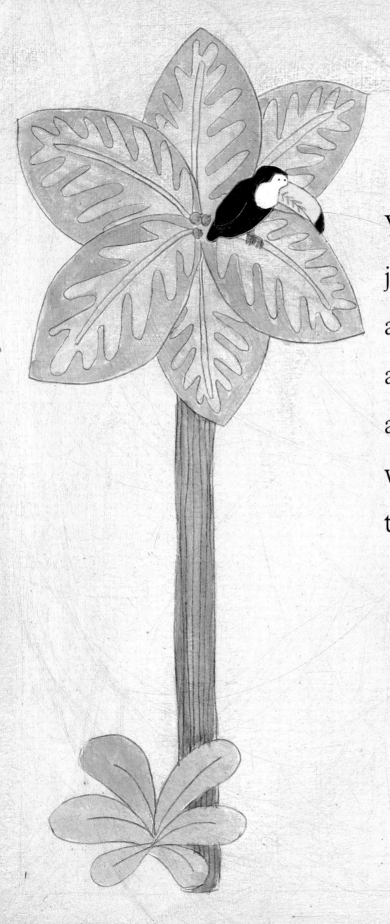

You might catch a glimpse
just now and then—
a flash of feathers from
a cockatoo,
a glint of fur where tigers
weave their trails among
the trees.

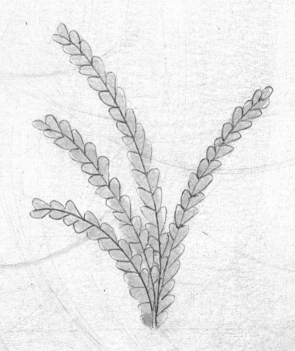

All the time, of course,
you know they're there.
But when you catch them
in the corners of your eyes,
pretend you don't.

Wild things like to take
you by surprise.
What they like best is
creeping up on YOU.

They're curious too.
Don't look behind you.

Sneak quietly beneath
the vines.
Creep silently among
the undergrowth.
Be very careful where
you put your feet.
There may be a crocodile
behind that log.

But then, down here,
where the pool
is still and clear,
here's where
the gentlest animals
come down to drink.

You can almost feel them
bending down around you.
You can almost see them
in the water.

Don't look up.
Wait very quietly.
Half close your eyes.

They gather in their dozens
and their hundreds
and their herds and tribes
and great, gigantic families.

Just sniff and listen.
Feel their shadows.
Squint your eyes.

When they're gone,
you somehow
sort of know.

Going back,
the path
is always shorter.

When you come
out of the jungle
into the open,
don't you feel like . . .

running, jumping,
crashing, thumping,
stamping down and
dancing around and
shouting!

JUDY HINDLEY is the author of more than thirty books for children, including *The Big Red Bus, A Piece of String Is a Wonderful Thing,* and *The Wheeling and Whirling-Around Book.* She dedicated *Into the Jungle* to her aunt and her father because, she says, "they both were spellbinding storytellers."

MELANIE EPPS exhibits her paintings in galleries in the United States, England, and Japan. She found illustrating *Into the Jungle,* her first book for children, "exciting—and magical—because it is the child's imagination that creates the story."